Libraries & Archives

Please return on or before the latest date above.
You can renew online at www.kent.gov.uk/libs
or by phone 08458 247 200

SCARLETT & CRIMSON

DarqStarz Rising

by Allyson Black
illustrated by Patrick Spaziante

SIMON AND SCHUSTER

SIMON AND SCHUSTER
First published in Great Britain in 2009 by Simon & Schuster UK Ltd,
1st Floor, 222 Gray's Inn Road, London WC1X 8HB
A CBS Company

Originally published in the USA in 2009 by Simon Spotlight, an imprint of Simon & Schuster
Children's Division, New York.

This book was written in collaboration with David Cody Weiss and Bobbi JG Weiss

A CIP catalogue record for this book is available from the British Library

ISBN 978-1-84738-619-9

10 9 8 7 6 5 4 3 2 1

Printed and bound in United States of America

www.simonandschuster.co.uk
www.scarlettandcrimson.com

SUNDAY

"Crimson? You down here?" Scarlett Ravencraft yelled into the shadows beyond the wine cellar rooms.

"In the Lair!" Crimson Hawthorne shouted back.

Scarlett's boots scuffed down the stone stairs. She turned right at the bottom, away from the dusty wine bottles and toward a dimly lit room at the end of a long hall. The floor of the room was covered in layers of throw rugs, and the ceiling and walls were artfully draped with printed fabrics. A couch and a comfy chair circled a beat-up old table. In one corner Crimson sat at a desk, moving images around on a computer screen.

"Stop what you're doing, Cee. I've got a major news alert for you."

"No can do, Ess," Crimson said, not looking away from the screen. "I'm just putting the last pieces together on *DarqSpace*. I already put our profiles in, see?"

SCARLETT RAVENCRAFT

" . . . it's all about Darqness."

BASICS

Interests:	Music, fashion, style, stark landscapes & hidden wonders
Sign:	Cancer
Pets:	Ruby Moon, Queen of Cats
Top 5 Friends:	Crimson, Kaitlyn, Emzie, Tara, Garrett
Heroes:	Crimson
Talents:	Singing, rockin' out, fashion design
Ambition:	2 establish Darq as a major scene 2 help others conquer their fears and dare to be themselves

MEDIA

Music:	Presumed Innoncence, the Solos, tattootu, Some Assemblage ReQuired
Instruments:	Voice, any stringed instrument, not brass tho— numbz lipz
Movies:	*Nightmare B4 Xmas, C-Tube*

CRIMSON HAWTHORNE

Interests: Music, cosmic mysteries, style & music. Did I mention music?
Sign: Scorpio
Pets: Sir Baskerville Curmudgeon, Royal Scotty
Top 5 Friends: Scarlett, Kaitlyn, Emzie, Tara, Garrett
Heroes: Scarlett
Talents: Great harmony, rockin' out, thinking deep thoughts, marveling @ mysteries
Ambition: 2 establish Darq as a major scene 2 help others conquer their fears and dare to be themselves

BASICS

"Be your own scene."

MEDIA

Music: Some Assemblage Required, Innocent Evil, the Solos, tattootu
Instruments: Drums, drums, drums, guitar, keyboard, bass, voice
Movies: *Nightmare B4 Xmas*, silent movies, Homebrew Films

"Cool," said Scarlett, "but—"

Crimson waved her quiet. "Now I need you to help write a description of what our site is about to put on the home page."

"Simple—it's about Darqness."

"That's not enough. How about we say it's like

noticing the things that get overshadowed—overlooked by, like, almost everybody?"

Scarlett thought about it. "Great point. Gotta mention that everyone lives in their own Darq—alone—but not really because you know that you're not the only one alone. It's more like being alone together—it gives us the strength. It helps me be me, *my* way. And speaking of loners, I met—"

"I'm not sure that makes complete sense," Crimson muttered as she typed away. "But it sounds good, I guess. What about music?"

"DarqStyle, of course. Not that many bands know that's what they're playing—but they will after *we* review them. Music with strong emotions and deep lyrics that's still totally danceable. Music that attracts kindred souls—and *speaking* of kindred souls—"

Without looking away from the screen, Crimson said innocently, "I'm totally guessing here, but are you trying to tell me something?"

"Ya think?" Scarlett shot back.

Crimson turned to face her friend. "So? S'up?"

"I just saw the new transfer student down at the mall," Scarlett bubbled. "Have you *seen* him yet?"

"British? Shades welded to his head? Blue streak-job hair? Totally anime? Goes by the name Pepper White? Has a minicamera attached to his hand twenty-four/seven?" Crimson said. "Nope. Haven't laid eyes on him."

Scarlett sniffed loudly. "We need to get you some glasses, girl." Ideas started pouring into her head. "Yeah . . . black ones, the pointy kind. Maybe bat wing frames . . ."

Crimson interrupted her friend's design trance. "I can see clearly enough to know he's fresh meat for the Leetz sharks. Those girls will chew him up, swallow him, and then—"

"Serve him up in school as Friday's mystery meat!" they finished together. "Eww!"

Grabbing control of the conversation, Scarlett said, "Back on topic, Cee, I really think Pepper White's got Darq potential."

Crimson looked up from under her black bangs. "Do you really think we've got a shot at even *talking* to him with the Leetz pack stalking him?"

Scarlett plopped into an overstuffed chair. "He's a *band geek*, Cee! We're bound to run into him in music class, if not in the practice room."

For the first time Crimson perked up. "And he plays what?"

Scarlett waved her arms around in excitement. "Anything, as far as I know. But he's got mad skills with keyboards and computers, from what I hear." She stared at her friend. "Trust me on this one?"

"I'll decide after I meet him," Crimson said firmly. She cocked a skeptical eyebrow. "If you think he's Darq material, how are you gonna beat the Leetz to him?"

Scarlett allowed herself to look smug. "I'm a Ravencraft. Trained from the womb to get what I want. Have I ever let us down?"

Crimson fell to her knees and bowed to Scarlett. "You're right. I should never have dissed the Scarlett Steamroller."

Scarlett waved a regal dismissal.

Crimson scrambled back into her seat, her eyes gleaming. "I get it now. It's a challenge! I'm in." She spun back around to the screen. "Now we've got *that* settled, let's finally get back to *my* topic. We're supposed to be explaining the Mysteries of the Darq to people who come to our site. We only have three weeks before Halloween, and I want to make a splash before then."

"What have you got so far?"

Crimson pointed at the monitor.

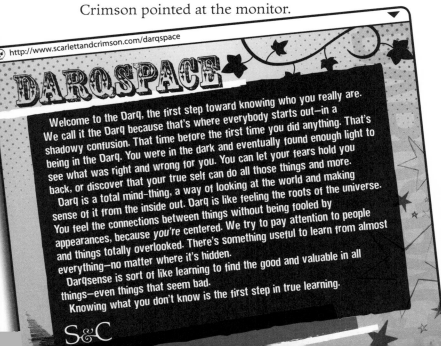

http://www.scarlettandcrimson.com/darqspace

DARQSPACE

Welcome to the Darq, the first step toward knowing who you really are. We call it the Darq because that's where everybody starts out—in a shadowy confusion. That time before the first time you did anything. That's being in the Darq. You were in the dark and eventually found enough light to see what was right and wrong for you. You can let your fears hold you back, or discover that your true self can do all those things and more.

Darq is a total mind-thing, a way of looking at the world and making sense of it from the inside out. Darq is like feeling the roots of the universe. You feel the connections between things without being fooled by appearances, because *you're* centered. We try to pay attention to people and things totally overlooked. There's something useful to learn from almost everything—no matter where it's hidden.

Darqsense is sort of like learning to find the good and valuable in all things—even things that seem bad.

Knowing what you don't know is the first step in true learning.

S&C

"Even if all you learn is, '*Never do this again!*'" Scarlett snarked.

"I'm not going to put that in," Crimson said primly. Then she broke into a smile. "Even if it does seem to be the only way some people learn."

Scarlett started getting hyper again. "Darq is, like, totally brain changing! It can turn all your glooms into glads, it can—"

"Cure zits, yeah," finished Crimson. "Save it for the infomercial."

"Well, it does have the coolest music to express it all: our band!" said Scarlett, waving at the array of instruments along the other side of the room.

"Which we *still* don't have a name for, by the way," said Crimson with a sigh.

"Got that covered, Cee," Scarlett said bouncily. "I've got the most totally Darq name for our band: DarqEssence!"

"And this is better than the other twenty-three names you've come up with *how*?"

"Because not only does it say that Darq is, like, totally vital, but it's actually got our initials in it—Ess and Cee!" Scarlett threw herself out of the chair and wrapped her arms around Crimson. "How cool is that?"

Crimson blew Scarlett's black hair out of her face. "Wouldn't it be pronounced DarqEssen*cee*, then?"

Scarlett flounced away. "Picky, picky. At least *I'm* coming up with names."

"Only 'cause you can't settle on one and then stick with it."

Scarlett's cell phone rang with the opening hook for the Questionable Muffins's latest download, "Raisins R Humiliated Grapes." When she pushed the speaker button, Mrs. Fleur Ravencraft's voice threatened sweetly, "If you don't come up and feed Ruby Moon *right now*, she'll knock over all the spices—again. And this time I'll make *you* realphabetize them. Hello, Crimson dear. Good-bye, Crimson dear."

"And she's the one who doesn't believe cats can tell time," Scarlett said as she flipped her phone closed.

Scarlett's Victorian-style house sat on a huge hill overlooking a suburban valley that used to be farm and ranch land. When Scarlett's dad built the house, he discovered an abandoned mine in the hill. Being a creative sort, he put a new door on the mine entrance at the foot of the hill and converted some of the chambers into rooms for his wine cellar. An elevator ran from the kitchen down to the tunnels. And like Scarlett's brother, Skip, had done before them, the girls had claimed one of the rooms as their secret hideaway. Because Crimson's house was only a quarter mile from the ground-level entrance, she could meet her friend any time without having to bike a mile out of her way to get to Scarlett's hilltop house.

The girls split up as they left the Lair, Scarlett heading for the freight elevator that would take her back up to the kitchen while Crimson headed for the delivery door and her home beyond.

"Well, I like DarqEssence for our band name! At least sleep on it to give it a chance, Cee!" Scarlett called as she stepped into the elevator. "Night!"

"Deal!" Crimson called back. "Night!"

Behind them in the room, the computer monitor flickered, broadcasting a message of hope into the shadows.

I hate, hate, hate, hate, hate, hate, hate, hate, Mondays

"I hate, hate, *hate* Mondays," Crimson complained as she and Scarlett hustled through the halls of V. Price Memorial Middle School between classes. "Not just for the regular reasons, but because I hardly get to see you. Sure, we have music together, but Ms. Chelle had us rehearsing from minute one. You got any idea what her big announcement tomorrow is about?"

Scarlett shook her head. The rest of her was vibrating as streams of walking students parted around her.

"Okay." Crimson sighed. "Out with it, before you explode."

"The Leetz pounced on Pepper White at lunch today!" Scarlett blurted out breathlessly.

Crimson frowned at the news. "And losing our chance to talk to him first is good *how*?"

"It's good because you couldn't be wronger!" Scarlett squealed happily. "The Leetz got totally owned! It was like extra dessert, watching those snotty attitudes get squished!"

"Those being . . . ?"

"Y'know, the hard-cores—Brianna, Paige, Kellie, Marissa, Brooke, and their pet jester, Casey," Scarlett explained. "They were all hanging in Leetz Corner when Pepper came cruising in, talking to Winslow

Leek. Guess they bonded in computer lab or something. Anyway, Paige and Brianna made like Winslow wasn't even there and vamped up to Pepper to honor him with an invitation. Pepper was, like, in that great accent of his, 'I am assuming my new friend is invited too?' Of course, Paige had to lecture him like he was part of their airhead tribe: 'The whole point of being exclusive is that we get to *exclude* people.' Can you believe it? She was all, like, why would you want to hang with Leaky Louie here when you could hang with *us*?"

Crimson shook her head. "Her honesty would be refreshing if it wasn't so bonehead stupid."

"So anyway," Scarlett continued, "Pepper just arched an eyebrow under his bleached swoop and said, superdry-like, 'Sorry, I don't dump my friends just for a posse upgrade.' Then he and Winslow staked out a windowsill as their turf and geeked out for the rest of lunch!"

Crimson was impressed. "Cool. No guy has ever resisted Paige's spray-on charm. We should tell the biology teacher. Maybe we could duplicate whatever he's got and give the boys immunity shots or something."

The warning bell cut off any further conversation.

"Catch you online after school!" Crimson shot back over her shoulder as she raced for class.

"Totally!" Scarlett called back.

Crimson stepped out onto the lawn as she left school. She inhaled deeply and soaked up the signs of the oncoming fall. Leaves were changing colors. According to her science teachers, all those bright reds and yellows were always there in every leaf. They just got hidden under the green color of chlorophyll. Then, when trees went to sleep for the winter, the chlorophyll faded, so the reds and yellows suddenly showed through.

Lots of stuff turned out to be different from what you thought it was at first, she thought.

A voice with an English accent broke her Darq thoughts. "Ah! Crimson Hawthorne! Just who I wanted to see. Leek said I'd probably find you here."

Crimson turned to see the lanky figure of Pepper White looming over her. A minicamera with a blinking red light was in his hand.

"Huh, me?" Crimson babbled, feeling silly. But he'd come out of nowhere!

Pepper grinned at her. "Aha! Speechless—and captured for eternity on video."

"You're *filming* me?"

"You noticed," Pepper said. "Yes. Me. Film. You. Digital video, actually. I am the camera. The camera is me. Don't mind me. Just act normally."

"That'll be the day," Crimson answered. "Or so Scarlett says. Constantly. Spit! Now you've got *me* talking in choppy bits."

"It's contagious, I know," said Pepper with a perky grin. He looked around. "Is your shadowy twin about? I have a little plan I think you might fancy signing up for."

"Uh . . . we make it a rule never to sign things," Crimson said cautiously. "We like to make our own decisions."

"Exactly!" Pepper said. "Leek tells me that you've

got a totally different take on music." He checked out Crimson's outfit. "And on fashion as well, I see. Leek likes you," Pepper added. "He's been recording your practice sessions. He gave me a copy." Pepper held up a hand-labeled CD. "I like what you do. I want to set up a bit of a jam to see if our tastes run the same way."

Now Crimson was intrigued. "What do you play? Are you any good?"

"Anything with a keyboard in answer to query one, and brilliant in answer to query two," Pepper said proudly. "I often sing on key. Modestly, I also have mad mystical powers over tech. My dad's the guy who scaled down an entire mobile recording studio to the size of a fridge. Turns just about any room into a top-flight digital recording suite. He's tinkering with those electronics tycoons over in the industrial park to kick-start mass production. Which is what brings me to the great American Heartland—and your fascinating musical style."

"Well, I can't make decisions for Scarlett, but I'm sure we can talk about it," said Crimson. Then she took a deep breath and blurted, "Hey, we just started our DarqSpace web page. Why don't you log on tonight, and you can ask her yourself?"

Pepper took down the site's URL. "Brilliant! We'll chat this evening then."

Later that evening Crimson filled Scarlett in on her encounter with Pepper as they chatted online.

DarqChat with Scarlett, Crimson, and Pepper
@ 8:23 p.m. on Monday

C He had a disc that Winslow burned of R music & said he wanted 2 jam & see if we clicked.

S Sounds way cool. But Cee, UR already R keyboard player! We don't need 2!

C I can shift 2 drums long enuf 2 hear his chops, Ess. Let's book time w/ Ms. Chelle tomorrow. What's 2 lose? Let's try it @ least.

P Is this a priv8 convo, or can any1 who can transl8 American in2 proper English join in?

S U invited him 2 post here already?

**DarqChat with Scarlett, Crimson, and Pepper
@ 8:38 p.m. on Monday**

C O, yeah. I didn't get 2 that point in the story yet. Welcome 2 DarqSpace, Pepper.

P Delighted! BTW, I took the liberty of preparing my profile 2 add 2 the site.

P ## Pepper White
Interests: Music, computers, music, video, music, being the still at the center of everybody's storms, taking notes
Sign: Virgo
Top 5 Friends: All imaginary
Heroes: Directors, especially Guillermo Del Toro, the Wachowskis, Miyazaki, and of course, me
Talents: Singing, rockin', N creating things nobody else has ever thought of
Ambition: 2 rule the world, natch. Don't worry, I'll take care of it
Music: the Solos; the New Originals; Dregs of Empire; Puddin' 4 Breakfast; Lean Against the Machine; the Questionable Muffins; Whale Omelette; the Smitfits
Instruments: If it has a keyboard, I play it
Movies: Viral videos; *Sweeney Todd*; *Nightmare B4 Xmas*; anything Monty Python; Spaced; English films nobody's ever heard of

S Looks cool.

C Seconded.

S BTW, Pepper, we R both onboard 4 a jam 2morrow in the Music Suite.

P Brilliant! C U then. Gotta run now!

Seánie's father, Gabe Barolli Jr, was a home builder and started his workday at six a.m. sharp.

TUESDAY

Scarlett's father, Gabe Ravencraft, was a home builder and started his workday at six a.m. sharp every day of the year, Christmas and New Year's included. Crimson's dad, Nat Hawthorne, owned a hardware supply store and often kept similar hours. Sometimes the two men worked on projects together and, sensibly, carpooled. Practical men, they saw nothing wrong with dropping their girls off at school on the way to work—even if it was an hour and a half before school even started. If nothing else, they reminded the girls, homework that might have been "forgotten" could be finished.

This was not the problem it might have been. Ms. Chelle made sure that the Music Suite was open to anyone who wanted to practice or record demos whenever students could squeeze in the time during their busy school weeks. Music students like Scarlett and Crimson had special ID/passkeys. They stopped by Mr. Silbers, the head janitor, to swipe their IDs through his scanner.

Properly logged in, the girls headed for the Music Suite, where they were totally floored to discover Pepper and Winslow already working there. Winslow was underneath the mixing board, fighting to impose order on a dense tangle of wires.

"It's no big deal," Pepper said about being in so early. "I'm still running on Greenwich Mean Time. My backbrain thinks dawn was six hours ago."

Winslow climbed to his feet. "The adapters are set, Pepper. You can patch in now."

"Morning, Winslow," Scarlett said cheerily.

Winslow actually blushed. He mumbled a return greeting and dove back into the safety of the wiry jungle.

The girls got their instruments from their lockers while Pepper snapped open the latches on what looked like a five-foot-wide fishing tackle box. The layers unfolded to create a horseshoe of seven keyboards, locked into place like a drum kit. Pepper tweaked the arrangement until he could stand in one place and reach any keyboard just by turning. He grinned at the girls. "One of the bennies of being my dad's son," he said. "I get to test out all the prototypes he comes up with."

He lit the boards up and hit the opening lick from Puddin' 4 Breakfast's hit "Why Not?" The girls joined in by the second line, with Winslow running a beat box in place of a drummer. Within minutes all three were improvising and passing licks back and forth. It was clear that there was a musical connection that caught up the players and, for a while, created a single sound that was more than just a jam session.

"Not bad," Ms. Chelle said from the doorway. "Not bad at all. And maybe just in time, too." She paused. "I'm going to announce it later today, but I might as well tell you now. The new Old Mill Rec Center is sponsoring a Battle of the Bands. There will be two judging rounds—one for demos, and a Battle of the Bands between the selected finalists from the whole school district. Any student group from Price Middle School can submit a CD demo of one song this Friday for judging this Saturday. The Battle will be held at the rec center's Halloween party." Ms. Chelle wrinkled her nose. "Thanks to the overwhelming boy vote, this year's theme will be Zombies versus Ninjas."

She shook that image out of her mind and focused on the girls. "I think you should work on a demo song together. Just a suggestion." With that, she unlocked her office and went inside.

"I'm game if you are," Pepper said. "But I don't have any songs of my own. Do you?"

"Umm," said Crimson.

Scarlett punched her friend in the shoulder. "Don't

give him that, Cee. You're always writing songs. You've got to have *tons* of stuff for us to choose from."

"Us?" Crimson answered, surprised.

"Of course," Scarlett said. "Didn't we just prove we have a groove that rocks? Why not run with it?"

"Let me think about it," Crimson said as the bell rang and she headed off to homeroom.

At lunch, Scarlett and Crimson sat with their usual posse—Kaitlyn, Emzie, Tara, and Garrett. Like always the talk was all about music, styles, and scenes. Scarlett was filling the others in about how designs just paraded through her head, like she was connected to this fashion cable broadcast no one else could see. She was serious about it and often talked about making design her major so she could see her visions brought to life.

Then across the cafeteria, Scarlett caught sight of Pepper leaving the serving line, Winslow in tow. But before he could even start looking for a place to sit, the Leetz surrounded him. Scarlett alerted the rest of the table to the ploy Paige, Kellie, Brianna, and Marissa were trying to pull. They weren't surprised that the Leetz were fawning over Pepper. The odd thing was that they were also giving Winslow the favor of their attention.

"I heard about your cool keyboard and your fresh sound," gushed Brianna, taking the lead in the Leetz's Grab for the New Guy.

"And I hear Ms. Chelle thinks you've got mad mixing skills—professional engineer, like," said Marissa to Winslow while flipping her bouncy hair. Winslow, turtlelike, tried to retract his head into his shirt. His eyes refused to meet Marissa's.

"Have you heard about the Battle of the Bands contest?" Paige said as she slid next to Pepper. "We're putting together a band to enter the contest because we're, like, the best at everything."

"Yeah, it's totally like our *duty* to ace this contest," Kellie declared.

Brianna said smugly, "And we figured that the best people—us—deserve the best backup crew around."

"With you working your keyboard magic and Winston filling out our sound . . ." Marissa groped for a way to express herself. Finally she just shrugged and said, "Well, let's just say that nobody else should risk the total humiliating *failure* of trying to compete with us."

"Best of all," Brianna summed up, "you get to be part of the Leetz scene."

"You must really be hard up to ask for help. This must mean a lot to you," Pepper drawled with a slight smirk. "By the way, points for almost remembering that Leek's given name is Winslow."

"We're winners," Brianna said matter-of-factly. "We do whatever we have to do to keep us winning. If that means *hiring* you and your nerdy friend, well, we'll suffer. First rehearsal is tonight. We'll audition you, and if you're good enough, you're in."

"Ah . . . sorry, but my time is booked," Pepper said. "Maybe sometime next century."

The Leetz stared in shock at Pepper. "You're working with *them*?" Marissa said with a curled lip as she glared Scarlett and Crimson's way. The rest of the Leetz wheeled to stare daggers at the two girls.

"As a matter of fact, yes," said Pepper cheerily.

"What. Ever." Brianna dismissed Pepper and turned to Winslow, leaning in close enough to fog his brain with her perfume. "What about you, tech boy? Want to join the Leetz?"

Winslow apparently lost the power of speech at that moment. His mouth worked, but no sound came out. Pepper came to his rescue. "He's not ready to make a commitment yet," Pepper said as he gripped Winslow by the shoulders and pulled him back from Marissa's personal Distraction Zone. "He'll get back to you on that one later."

The Leetz exchanged looks of frustration, then all turned at once and retreated to their table. Pepper steered Winslow over to Scarlett and Crimson's table. "Well," he said as he sat Winslow down and pulled out a chair for himself. "They certainly looked like they'd been hit by a bus. Hasn't anyone ever told them *no* before?"

"If so, they haven't lived to tell about it," Scarlett snickered.

"We're really going to do this," said Crimson, staring into space.

"Absolutely," Pepper said with complete authority. "Now, one of you mentioned that you've got the perfect rehearsal space."

"Me," said Scarlett. "We've got the Lair."

"Cool. Where's that?"

"Oh, you'll see," Scarlett said. "Come by Crimson's

house at about three o'clock and she'll lead you into our underground haven of Darqness."

"Sounds mysterious," Pepper said with a grin. "I love it already!"

Pepper pulled his scooter-and-trailer combo up to the last house on the dead-end street.

TUESDAY *Evening*

Pepper pulled his scooter-and-trailer combo up to the last house on the dead-end street. Before him towered a steep hill, and just visible over the top edge of it was a sprawling house.

Crimson was standing in her driveway. Her house was a lot smaller than the one at the top of the hill, but it had a comfy feel. "I'd invite you in," she told Pepper, "but the place is a mess. Dad works a lot, and I, uh, majorly fail at housekeeping. Anyway, we have to hurry around back to get to the graveyard."

"Graveyard?" Pepper said, his eyebrows high on

his forehead. "Oh, this just keeps getting better and better." He locked his bike to a tree and unhooked the lightweight trailer. Unattached, the trailer became a big carrying case on two wheels, with the scooter hookup becoming a handle. Towing the case behind him, Pepper followed Crimson around the house and down a dirt path leading toward the hill. The path soon passed a wrought-iron gate that fenced off dozens of marble headstones.

"This is the oldest graveyard in town," Crimson said. "My mom's buried right over there," she added, pointing. "On nights when I can't sleep, I come down here and talk to her. She's a great secret-keeper."

The dirt path soon joined a paved road that ended at the old mine entrance. Crimson swiped a plastic key card through an electronic lock and the new door rolled up. After she and Pepper entered, the door rolled back down, leaving them at the end of a well-lit hallway.

"Used to be a mine," said Crimson over her shoulder. As she led Pepper

past rock-walled chambers holding racks of dusty bottles, she explained how Scarlett's dad had built the wine cellar. "But there are other rooms and tunnels down here—*secret* rooms," she finished mysteriously.

Crimson stopped before a sturdy door with another swipe-card lock, which she opened. "Welcome to the Lair."

Pepper took one look at the amazing things in the room and his heart skipped a beat. First of all, the whole space was soundproofed with a dull black foam under all the nice fabrics the girls had pinned up. Second, there were instruments everywhere—several electric guitars, an electric bass, a keyboard, and an enormous drum

kit that had more traps and cymbals than Pepper had ever seen. Several microphones on stands clustered in one corner. The cozy corner of the room had a beat-up couch, a couple of beanbag chairs, a minifridge, and a microwave. There was a computer station off to one side. Drawings of fashion designs and doodles were pinned all over the place. One striking pencil drawing showed a large, stark, heart shape made out of two flocks of flying creatures coming out of the center. The left flock became butterflies and the right flock became bats.

"I'd love to say that Crimson and I created all this, but it's actually my big brother's work," Scarlett said, coming out from the computer station in the back. "Skin got into music for a while. And, being Skip, he bought all the equipment he thought he might need, set up this studio, and then lost interest six months later. He's planning on being a computer genius this week."

Not to be one-upped, Pepper pushed his trailer into the middle of the room. "Well, this is your lucky day, ladies. I've got the perfect match to this perfect room." He opened the trailer like a shell to reveal carefully packed electronic units. Within minutes, he had assembled a complete sound-recording board. "The Solo Portable Studio!" he declared, flashing a big-toothed grin.

He dug into the bottom of the trailer for a handful of radio transmitter packs. "So. Tell me who's playing what and I'll patch things in. I claim keyboard."

"Uh, we haven't settled on anything," Crimson said. "We usually just mess around on whatever instrument we pick up."

"Yeah, 'cause you can never make up your mind till the last minute," snarked Scarlett.

Crimson ignored her. "We saw videos of a cool duo that played only drums and guitar. We've been doing that kind of thing for a couple of weeks, with me on drums and Scarlett bouncing back and forth between bass and lead guitar."

With Pepper on the keyboard, they tuned up and began playing simple tunes to get in sync. When they hit their groove, they moved up to trying a couple of current hits. An electric current seemed to connect them, pushing them and the music further and further. Finally they abandoned playing straight tunes and just started improvising—throwing musical moves back and forth among the instruments.

After a good hour, they took a break and threw themselves down on the couch and beanbags. "Wow! That was awesome!" Scarlett said.

"That was true Darq music," declared Crimson, her eyes wide and sparkling. "It started low and moody, and then it got big and proud. Woot!"

"Darq," Pepper said thoughtfully. "Is that what you're calling it? Catchy hook, that."

"Oh, Darq is more than just the music, it's a whole new scene," Crimson said, jumping up from the couch. "Come check out our website for the whole skinny!"

"I wish I could go back and listen to us play again," Scarlett said dreamily.

"Thanks to my gear, you can," said Pepper. "Every note was recorded as we played it. Leek and I can polish it up and process it any way you want from here. I'll leave you MP3s of it before I go."

"Cool!" said Crimson. "Can we play it back now?"

"Tomorrow," said Scarlett as the clock caught her eye. "Right now I have to kick you both out and go upstairs for dinner. See you at school."

Wednesday seemed to fly by for Scarlett and Crimson. Their minds were on the evening's recording session, and the rest of the day was a blur of talking teachers and quick hellos passed in the hallways.

Immediately after school, Scarlett, Crimson, and Pepper gathered at the Lair and spent an hour warming up. They took a breather, sprawling across the furniture with a playback of their first jam playing softly in the background. Everyone had a cup of juice.

"Help a fellow out with something, would you?" said Pepper, putting his cup carefully on the rug.

"Sure," Scarlett and Crimson said in unison.

Pepper unfolded himself from the chair and got up. He fidget-walked around as he said, "Clearly, with Leek and the Leetz, as well as others I won't mention, I keep acting left-footed. It's a social minefield out there. Not that my old schools were free of that," he added hastily. "But a lot of that was class-clash. Here I'm completely clueless. I could use the advice of a couple of native guides on this."

Scarlett and Crimson exchanged a look. "Well, unfortunately, the first rule seems to be, like, *you* are your *scene*," said Scarlett.

"Who you are and what you think comes later, if ever," added Crimson with a disgusted shrug.

"And it's a rule somewhere that all scenes look down on all other scenes," finished Scarlett. "Cee and I think that's dumb, but that's how it goes."

Pepper, relaxed now, plopped back into a beanbag. "So what are the V. Price Memorial scenes?"

Crimson cocked her head. "Do you want to start from the top down, the bottom up, or from the extremes to the middle?"

Pepper's eyes brightened with interest. "Extremes

to the middle sounds like it would be wonderfully odd. I'll have that, please."

Scarlett took a deep breath. "'Okay, see, the ranking is totally by popularity. The top scenes brag about their high numbers, and the other scenes consider low numbers as a plus to their coolness score. They're, like, 'There's only a few special kids like us who have the *real* cool scene and all.'" Scarlett held her hand up at head level. "At the top of the food chain you've got the jocks and the Leetz, which are overlapping groups."

"Think gorillas and sharks partying in the same swimming pool," volunteered Crimson.

Pepper nodded. "I know the types. We have yobs and snobs back home, I assure you. Not the kind I'd hang about with."

"You can tell the populars because they herd-shop," said Scarlett. "They all go for whatever is on the Gotta Have list. You know, texting cell phones, the hot MP3 player of the moment, brand-name clothes. You can tell the real pops from the wannabes because the real Leetz have *two* of everything on the New Hotness list. What's the latest trend, Cee?"

"During school everybody has to lug around a

bookbag or backpack. The New Hot for girls is fuzzy cute animal backpacks. Extra points if it's an endangered species. The jocks and tough-guy wannabes have testosterone-positive canvas satchels. A tough guy on TV uses one, so that makes it manly."

"With us so far?" Scarlett asked Pepper.

He nodded, grinning with fascination.

"Okay. Now, down in the social swamp are all the *rebel* groups, the punks, the goths, the ravers, and the emos. The one thing every scene agrees on is that the emos are the lowest of the low. And get this—the emos eat it up, 'cause it, like, totally feeds their self-alienation. Go fig."

"Poor suffering emos. Spoil their day—give them a hug," snarked Crimson.

Scarlett made a rough swoop with her hand. "There's also a halo of Terminally Lame kids who just don't fit in anywhere. But they don't have any particular music."

"See, music is the key," Crimson explained. "That's the most important thing of all. Every scene has its

own music. Jocks are into metal, and the Leetz go with the flavor of the month."

"The punks and the ravers have similar tastes in music," Scarlett mused, "except the ravers will dance to punk as well as grunge music while the punks are into the anger thing, so they only like angry music. Well, not just music. They're angry at *everything*, even if they have to invent stuff that ticks them off."

Crimson laughed. "There's even neo-punks now, split-offs who claim that old punks aren't hard-core enough. Now the goths . . . ," Crimson paused thoughtfully, "the goths are music and costume welded together, all of it intended to be pushed into people's faces. If you're a goth, you've got to wear leather and studded dog collars and jewelry stuck in uncomfortable parts of your body. When people's eyes bug out at them, it totally feeds their egos." She refilled her cup with more mango juice. "Mild goths and emos can be mistaken for each other. They both like lots of eye makeup. But their attitudes are totally different."

"Somebody said that emos want to die dramatically—," Scarlett began. "And the goths just want everyone *else* to die, period," Crimson finished.

"All drama-queen hype, of course."

"In the middle, you have Geek Central—the comp sci nerds, the hard-core computer gamers—often overlapping, of course," Scarlett went on. "Most of them are glassy-eyed zombies who think school is just here to interrupt their online lives, where they spend hours playing video games." She swiped a sip from Crimson's juice glass. "And last but not least, there's the band geeks. That's the only scene that treats its members as more or less equal, no matter what other scene they're into."

"Talent transcends phony barriers," Crimson chanted like a mantra.

Pepper sat back, his face thoughtful as he digested all this. "So where does your scene fit in?"

"Oh, we're totally outside of all that," said Scarlett with a wave of her hand. "They can all play their little games if they want. We just watch and don't take anything they say about us seriously. We're making a place where everyone is equal. That's what Darq is about—it's that place you stand every time you want to do something but doubt yourself. It's like the edge of the diving board, when you're scared about jumping out into space."

Crimson nodded. "We want all our Darqlings to light up their minds and see their real worth, and no matter what their scene tells them to do, they can define themselves."

"We've got to make it a scene that kids will want to join and learn that you can talk about your problems and no Darqling will repeat them to anyone else. Our motto is *'Your secret's safe with us,'*" said Scarlett.

"And, of course, we're totally committed to making music that supports this, keeping DarqSense spreading every time someone hears our stuff," finished Crimson.

Pepper raised an eyebrow. "And our new band's name is . . ."

"DarqStarz," Crimson said out of the blue.

Scarlett stared at her friend. "Huh?"

"Good name," said Pepper. "I like it. Quite an ambitious plan, too. Well, it's never too early to get started, me da always says." He headed for the keyboard. "What song do you have that you want to record for the demo?"

Crimson reluctantly fetched a folder from her bookbag. She distributed a sheet of paper to Scarlett and Pepper. "It's called 'A Light in the Darq,'" she said. "I'm not sure if it's finished yet or not."

A LIGHT IN THE DARQ

Be your own scene. Be your own scene.

Who are you when you're all alone in the Darq?
Nothing but you and your own beating heart?

Be your own scene. Be your own scene.

Without all the glam and the gear and the fear,
They'll see that you're just too smart.

Be your own scene. Be your own scene.

To follow the fish as they all school away,
Turning "blend in" into some kind of art.

Be your own scene. Be your own scene.
Be your own scene. Be your own scene.
You know you have the skill,
And you sure deserve the thrill,
By now you know the drill . . .
Be your own scene.

After reading it, Pepper nodded approvingly. "Sweet. How do you plan on playing it?"

"Real chunky on the chorus line." Crimson picked up a guitar and played a progression with each word backed by a heavy chord. "Then for the verses, I figured on something soft—keyboards making veils of sound to give it a spacey feel."

"Brilliant," said Pepper, standing up and rubbing his hands together. "Let's start working on it."

In the course of the next several hours, they sketched out a tune hung on a nice chord progression and, pleased with that work, set about fine-tuning the composition.

It took almost the whole night, but the song was finally starting to come together. After almost four hours of playing, the band was exhausted!

They decided to take a break when Scarlett noticed a flashing message on the computer screen. "Somebody's instant-messaging the website," she called out. Scarlett went over to click on the chat window. "It's Winslow!" she said in surprise. Everyone gathered around the screen to read the message.

W Hey guys—you there? I've got a problem & I've got nobody else 2 talk 2.

S Pepper & Crimson R here 2. Whatz the prob?

W I don't know how 2 xplain. I did something wrong & I feel bad about it.

S U can trust us, like it says @ the top of the page, YOUR SECRET'S SAFE WITH US.

W Well, U & Pepper have been nice 2 me. Much nicer than . . . this is 2 embarrassing. U sure U won't tell NE1?

S Cross R hearts.

W Well, the Leetz want me 2 do something bad 2 you.

S Why in the world would U do that?

W We'll, they're kinda like . . . blackmailing me.

S No way! What 4?

W U promise not 2 laugh @ me 4 being stupid?

S Putting people down is NOT what Darq is about. U can trust us.

W Okay. Well, Brianna promised me a kiss if I would hack the school computer 2 up her bf's grade. He would've passed NEway, but . . . she said she liked me. & I believed her. So I did it.

W Brianna told me 2 come backstage in the auditorium 2 collect my kiss. I went there & it was dark. Brianna called me & told me 2 kiss her thru the curtains. I did, & I got a kiss all right, but it was from a slobbery basset hound. All the Leetz were videoing me on their cell phones. They sent me the pix.

W Now they say they'll upload them 2 the Net if I don't do 2 things—master their demo 4 them and . . . pls don't B mad @ me . . . They want me 2 trash UR demo when I mix it.

W But U guys have been nice 2 me w/o making fun of me. What do I do?

Scarlett looked at Crimson and Pepper. "Looks like we've got our first Ask Dr. Darq advice posting," she said. "What's the Darq way out of this for him?"

"Point him to see the good things he is, and get him to realize he's tough enough inside to do the right thing, even if it totally scares him," said Crimson.

"Let me take this, if you don't mind," said Pepper. He sat down, and his fingers danced across the keys.

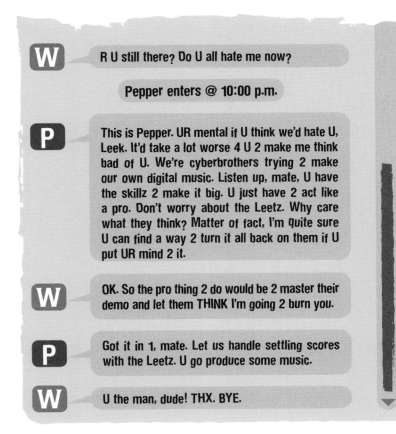

W R U still there? Do U all hate me now?

Pepper enters @ 10:00 p.m.

P This is Pepper. UR mental if U think we'd hate U, Leek. It'd take a lot worse 4 U 2 make me think bad of U. We're cyberbrothers trying 2 make our own digital music. Listen up, mate, U have the skillz 2 make it big. U just have 2 act like a pro. Don't worry about the Leetz. Why care what they think? Matter of fact, I'm quite sure U can find a way 2 turn it all back on them if U put UR mind 2 it.

W OK. So the pro thing 2 do would be 2 master their demo and let them THINK I'm going 2 burn you.

P Got it in 1, mate. Let us handle settling scores with the Leetz. U go produce some music.

W U the man, dude! THX. BYE.

"Cool," Pepper said as he logged off. "Leek is back on track. Hawthorne, Ravencraft"—he pointed at Crimson and Scarlett—"the first thing we do to smack down the Leetz is make a demo that'll blow everyone away."

By way of answer, Scarlett and Crimson headed back to their instruments and played the opening lick of "A Light in the Darq."

THURSDAY

Pepper and Winslow had become welcome members of Scarlett and Crimson's crowd at their usual table in the cafeteria, but today neither one was there. In fact, Crimson was missing as well, which made Scarlett feel holes in the conversations with Tara, Emzie, Kaitlyn, and Garrett where Crimson's dry, snarky comments would have had everyone doubled over with laughter.

Twenty minutes late, Crimson came racing into the cafeteria. She assembled her lunch in a blur and speed-walked to the table.

"So where were you?" Scarlett demanded. The rest of the posse focused on Crimson.

"With . . . mph . . . Pepper and Winslow . . ." Crimson forced herself to swallow, and then took a couple of big gulps of her drink. "They're mixing the song on the school board, and Pepper wanted me to do some guitar overdubs." She dove back into her lunch. "I've only got twenty minutes to eat so I can go back to the studio for more overdubs if Pepper needs them."

"No need, Hawthorne," said Pepper. It was as if he'd appeared out of nowhere, followed by his human shadow, Winslow.

"Leek and I have a decent rough mix here," he said as Winslow held up a thumb drive. "Who's got an MP3 player?"

Everyone had one, of course. One by one Winslow loaded each player with the music. Amid all the clamor of the cafeteria, one table became curiously quiet as the group listened to "A Light in the Darq." The only sound came from Crimson as she vacuumed her plate—but even she was listening to the recording as she ate.

Pepper stood perfectly at ease as the others reacted

to his work. Winslow, however, couldn't stop fidgeting. His eyes flicked from listener to listener, looking for a scowl or yawn. For Winslow, rejection was always just a frown away.

"Wow!" said Emzie. "That's just—"

"Totally amazing!" finished Garrett.

Tara looked impressed. "It sounds like the music is, I don't know, coming from *inside* me when I listen."

"The sound is so *deep*!" Emzie said. "Like it was recorded in a huge concert hall."

Winslow beamed like a puppy who'd just gotten praise instead of a scolding. "We can shape the sound envelope to mimic any space, from stairwell to stadium," he said shyly.

Pepper took the compliments in stride, of course. "The school's equipment is a bit primitive compared to a Portable Studio," he said, waving a long-fingered hand. "I want Hawthorne to rerecord her guitar tracks on her own guitar, and I think that Ravencraft and I should rework the bass track layering, but for a work in progress, it's coming along smartly."

Tara was swaying to the music as she replayed the song. "If this is what you're going to upload to your website, I've just got to check it out."

"Me too," said Kaitlyn, equally blissed out on the tune. "You got lyrics to this?"

"Laying down the vocals is this afternoon's project," Pepper said as Scarlett scribbled the web address on four strips of paper torn from her notebook and handed them out. "Then Leek and I will work our digital magic on it tonight and have a totally kick-butt demo to submit in music class tomorrow."

"Don't you have to work on the Leetz demo too?" said Crimson as she loudly slurped the last of her drink through the straw.

"Their stuff is so simple that I could mix it in my sleep," Winslow replied. His brow creased. "Actually, I think I *was* half-asleep when I mixed it late last night. Their band is pretty tight, but boy, do the girls' voices need a lot of filters to make them sound decent."

"What are they doing?" Scarlett asked.

"Well, they're doing a cover of Presumed Innocence's 'You Can't Prove I Did It,'" Winslow said. "But since Paige, Brianna, Marissa, Kellie, and Brooke can't play any instruments, they arm-twisted a few music geeks to back them with a four-piece band while they sing all together in front." He gave a snorting laugh. "Brianna and Paige keep trying to upstage each other and make the other Leetz look like backup singers."

The bell rang just then, cutting off any further secret reports on the Leetz and their demo. "See you this afternoon," Pepper said as he and Winslow strolled away.

Pepper had brought his expando-keyboard setup to the Lair. "The better to work my magic, fair ladies," he explained. "Actually, I prefer to use my gear if possible. It drives me mad to hear recordings that I know I could have done better."

Pepper's perfectionism showed. He had both Scarlett and Crimson do take after take on each instrument, hoping to catch a special magic in one of those performances. While Scarlett went upstairs for a snack tray, Pepper and Crimson put together the best tracks and poked and prodded them until they had the instrumentals for "A Light in the Darq" locked down enough to lay vocals over them.

When Scarlett returned, Pepper set the instrumentals to play on a loop while the three of them scarfed down sandwiches and fruit. The more they listened to the track, the more they liked how the song was shaping up.

They spent the rest of the evening arranging the vocals. With the Solo Portable Studio it was easy for them to do variations on who sang what part. They finally settled on Crimson doing the verses solo and all three belting "Be your own scene" in harmony.

During their next break the computer chimed, announcing an instant message being sent to the DarqSpace website. "That's probably Leek checking in to see how things are going," Scarlett said. She slid into the chair and tapped the keyboard to light up the sleeping screen.

W Bad news, guys. The Leetz are turning the thumbscrews on me. Now they not only want me 2 trash UR demo, they want me 2 erase all UR copies from the hard drive—except 4 1 CD. Like I'd ever do that 2 anybody, much less 2 U guys.

S What do they want with the 1 copy?

W Knowing them, they probably want it 2 wave in UR face & drive U nuts.

S BRB—Pepper's saying something.

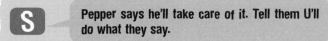

S Pepper says he'll take care of it. Tell them U'll do what they say.

W OK, I guess. BTW, thank Crimson 4 me. She gave me an idea 2day on how 2 take care of those stupid pictures of me. C ya!

Scarlett logged off and swiveled her chair to face Pepper. "You have something up your sleeve, don't you?"

"Ask me no questions and I'll tell you no lies," Pepper said. "Anyway, we don't have time to worry about the Leetz. It's time to put our noses to the grindstone. We have vocals to record!"

The moon was high in the sky when Crimson tiptoed out the back door. She didn't want to wake her father. Nat Hawthorne got up early and sometimes worked twelve-hour days. He was already snoring in his bedroom.

She made her way across the yard toward the track leading to the graveyard. When she reached the wrought-iron gate, she squeezed through a gap in the bars. Following a path she could have followed with her eyes closed, she navigated through the worn marble monuments with their cherubs and angels until she came to her mother's grave.

Carved into the headstone were the words,

Lenore Hawthorne
Beloved Wife & Mother
"To Live in the Hearts of Those You Love
Is Not to Die."

Crimson sat down on the grass. "Hi, Mom," she said to the headstone. "You'll never believe what happened this week." She gave her mother a rundown of everything that had happened since she and Scarlett had met Pepper White.

"It's like, a super rush and all, and I can totally get behind letting people know and think about Darq. But part of it scares me too. I mean, those are my words in that song. What if people love the music but hate the lyrics?

"*I* think it's good—better than that, I think the song is *great*!—but what if nobody else does? I always wanted to do something majorly important to help people. Darq'll do that, if we can get it viral.

"You're right. If I'm going to talk the talk, I've gotta walk the walk. What's the Darq answer to this? Throw myself into it and do the best I can."

Crimson stood up and patted the headstone gently. "You know, talking to you like this always makes me feel better. It's okay, but . . . I still really miss you."

With one last, lingering look, Crimson turned and headed back to her home and bed.

FRIDAY

On Friday morning, Ms. Chelle devoted the last ten minutes of the music class to collecting demos from the students who wanted to enter the contest. A crowd quickly surrounded her, holding CDs in carefully labeled cases. First in line, of course, were Brianna and Paige, the only two Leetz to actually take music class. The CD case Brianna handed in was bright pink with flower shapes drawn on in neon marker.

Scarlett and Crimson marched up together to hand Ms. Chelle their demo disc. They had taken special care in designing their label. Inspired by a sketch hanging

in the Lair, it was a heart made up of butterflies and bats against a bloodred background. It really caught the eye, and they heard a couple of hushed "wow's" behind them. As they returned to their seats, they could feel Brianna staring daggers at them.

Scarlett and Crimson exchanged a glance and had one of those telepathic moments all close friends share. In unison, they turned and gave their supersweetest social smiles at Brianna. She reddened and bit her lip to keep silent—Ms. Chelle tolerated no misbehavior in her class—then decided a return smile was the best comeback. Except her smile looked more like a snarl.

Scarlett and Crimson barely made it back to their seats without bursting out laughing.

Ms. Chelle called the class to order. In her hands she held the submitted discs. "I am *so* pleased that so many of you decided to offer your work for others to hear," she began. "I'll have Winslow upload all these to the judging website, and the best ten demos in the school district—in the opinion of the contest judges—will be selected and move on to the live round. Tomorrow those demos will be played in the auditorium, and the judges will explain their decisions." She walked over to Winslow sitting at the soundboard and handed him the stack of discs. He kept his head down and avoided looking at either Brianna or Scarlett and Crimson.

"For those of you whose work isn't chosen, don't take it too much to heart," Ms. Chelle added. "Music is as much taste as it is skill. You may not find an open audience in these judges, but if you work hard and ignore the times you don't win, sooner or later you will find your audience. Good luck and . . ."—the bell rang—"class dismissed."

While Brianna waited for the Music Suite to empty, two bulky football players entered. One was Brianna's boyfriend, Billy Tannen, who went by the nickname "Beef." She flicked her eyes at Winslow at the soundboard. She got up and, flanked by her goons, walked over to him.

"The disc," Brianna said, holding out her hand.

"Which disc is that?" mumbled Winslow.

Beef growled, and his pal cracked his knuckles loudly.

"The one you're supposed to make disappear," Brianna hissed. "Hand it over—or some really embarrassing pictures are gonna appear on every bulletin board, not to mention that Intertubes thingy."

Still not looking up, Winslow silently handed Brianna a bright red disc with a heart shape printed in black on the label. "And you wiped the files from Pepper's hard drive?"

"Mmph," Winslow replied.

Beef took Winslow's jaw in his massive hand and forcibly lifted Winslow's head. "Look at the chick when she's talkin' to you," he growled.

Winslow stared dead-eyed in Brianna's direction.

"No copies of that song remain on any hard drive. Not a single byte," he muttered. "I swear."

"Good," said Brianna. She sighed. "Isn't it amazing how easy things go when people simply do the things I tell them to?"

Brianna and her escorts left the Music Suite without a backward look. If they had, they'd probably have been very puzzled by the thin smirk on Winslow's face.

Scarlett and Crimson sat down at their lunch table alone. The rest of the posse were still in line. No sooner were their trays on the table when the royal court of the Leetz—Brianna, Paige, and Kellie—loomed over them. Behind them hovered Casey, looking for any opportunity to crack wise.

"Do you actually think your amateur moony music can beat our demo?" Brianna sneered.

"*You* outclass *our* stellar vocal performances?" Paige said with her nose in the air. "As if!"

Casey butted in. "Yeah, they got a pro band to back them. What did you guys use—a karaoke track?"

The Leetz girls shot Casey a dirty look. "You

weren't supposed to tell anybody about the band," snarled Brianna.

Casey was clueless. "Huh?"

Kellie dismissed the whole problem with a toss of her hair. "Well, why not admit it?" she said in a bored tone. "So we had a backing band instead of burdening ourselves with guitars. The music was only there to, like, support our totally incredible vocals. And it's not like these two are going to win anyway."

"And just why do you say that?" Crimson asked sweetly.

Paige smiled her most superior smile. "Let's just say that it's all down to the technical help you can attract." Her eyes flicked toward Winslow as he approached the table.

But then her smile turned troubled. Winslow was walking with Kaitlyn, Emzie, Tara, Pepper, and Garrett, and they all carried their trays with one hand. Despite his notorious shyness,

Winslow was surrounded by girls . . . and smiling. The others were laughing too—at sheets of paper they were carrying in their free hands.

When they all sat down at the table, Winslow flipped a few of the papers toward the Leetz. "I'm thinking of making it into a T-shirt," he said. "Wanna buy one?"

The Leetz stood frozen, staring down at the papers fanned out before them. The papers were copies of a blown-up photo of Winslow getting a slobbery kiss from a dog. But Winslow had Photoshopped Brianna's hair onto the dog and printed on the picture, "I Kissed a Leet—and Lived!!!"

Scarlett and Crimson doubled over trying to smother their laughter.

"So there goes your blackmail," Winslow said firmly to Brianna. "And by the way, I changed Beef's grade back to what it had been—as if anyone would believe he'd get an A plus in math."

Just then, a girl hardly anyone knew came up to the table carrying an MP3 player. "Your song is just *so* cool," she gushed to Scarlett and Crimson. "All my friends really love 'A Light in the Darq.' Thanks for uploading it for free to your website."

Brianna whirled on Winslow. "You said you wiped the song from their hard drive. You lied to us!"

"Nope," he answered. "I've been perfectly honest. Not a byte of Scarlett and Crimson's song remains on any hard drive." Winslow looked at the back of his hand and pursed his lips. "Of course, I might have burned a bunch of CDs and put it on the DarqSpace site *before* I erased the files on the HD. . . ."

He dug into his shirt pocket and produced a handful of mini-CDs, all printed with the bat/butterfly heart and red label. He offered them to the posse and put one into each outstretched hand. He held one out to the Leetz. "Want one?" Then he pulled the disc back. "Oh, that's right . . . you already have one, don't you? Too bad it's blank."

If glares could petrify, the Leetz would have turned the entire table into garden gnomes. Without another word, the dissed girls turned and stalked away.

Behind them trailed Casey, muttering, "What? What just happened?"

The girls cheered Winslow, and Pepper high-fived him. Winslow was a few microseconds slow and missed, but Pepper, laughing, tried it again. This time Winslow moved in sync, and their palms met in a satisfyingly solid slap.

FRIDAY Afternoon

By four o'clock, both Scarlett and Crimson were ready to chew their fingernails up to their elbows. They both agreed that the only way to break the tension of waiting for the judging was to head down to the Velvet Kiss.

Its full name was the Velvet Kiss Exotic Clothing Emporium, but nobody ever called it anything more than the Velvet Kiss, or TVK if they went there often. Situated in the oldest part of Old Mill, it was originally a large, Victorian-style house owned by one of the early mayors. Now it was home to twin sisters Flora and Fauna Hepburn, who had turned all the ground-floor rooms into a fantastic fabric bazaar. The twins themselves lived up in the upper stories, which meant TVK was open whenever the twins felt like it, day or night.

Almost anything could be found at the Velvet Kiss. The Hepburn twins sold fabric by the yard, of course, but that was almost a sideline to their real love—vintage clothes. Where else could anyone find the fringed skirt of a real 1920s flapper dress or one of those weird fluffy poodle skirts that were all the rage in the 1950s? There were whole outfits from every fashion period that had ever swept through Old Mill, and tons more shirts, pants, jackets, and swatches of exotic cloth. And that's not to mention jewelry—both costume and real. TVK was heaven for creative fashion fans.

Crimson climbed the front porch before Scarlett, but waited for her friend before opening the oversize double doors. Together they stepped into the entrance hall and stopped to inhale the wonderful

smells of the Velvet Kiss. Tiny threads of jasmine incense floated through the air. And each outfit on each of the mannequins standing in the entrance hall had its own unique smell too. That woolen jacket over there on the headless male mannequin had a fuzzy, dusty smell. By contrast, that taffeta party dress on the female mannequin next to it had a tickle-in-the-nose cotton candy scent. The girls stood enchanted, Crimson concentrating on the earthy smell of a leather raincoat,

Scarlett drinking in the whole array of aromas at once.

Finally they broke their trance and went into the big room—or, as the twins called it, the "parlor"—beyond the entrance hall. As usual, Flora and Fauna Hepburn were busy sorting clothes and arranging them on hangers. The twins not only kept the store in their house, but they often wore the clothes themselves.

Today one of them was wearing a shell-patterned blue Japanese kimono over a ruffled white linen shirt with a high, starched lace collar. A pair of number two pencils were stuck through her bun, keeping it not quite neatly in place. She looked weirdly regal compared to her twin, who was wearing a tan airline hostess's uniform from the nineties with the jacket retailored into a cute bolero, decorated with silver thread braiding. She had ironed glitter into the skirt so that it shimmered when she moved. Topping it all was an old orange pilot's hat that she wore at a sassy tilt. She had even put a strip of colored flashing LEDs around the hatband.

Both sisters, who were in their thirties, wore identical fire-engine-red tights on their legs. One was examining an antique wedding dress, while the other sat behind the desk they used as a sales counter.

"Welcome, welcome, welcome!" said the one in the kimono, with a cheery smile.

"So good to see you back," said the one in the uniform. "Did you bring us more designs? The last ones were really quite good, you know."

"Hi, Flora. Hi, Fauna," the girls chimed in unison. Scarlett answered the question. "No. Nothing new today. We just came to poke around, 'cause we're so nervous about the demo contest."

"How lovely," said Kimono. "We wish you good luck, of course."

"We always knew you two were special," said Uniform. "Just like everyone knew we were special when we were your age."

"So go ahead, poke around all you want," said Kimono. "We just got some lovely costumes from a theater that closed. They're in the dining room."

"If you need any help," added Uniform, "just holler and Flora or I will come."

"Wait a minute," Kimono said to her twin.

"*You're* Flora, aren't you? I mean, I've been calling you that all day."

"Maybe I am," said Uniform, tapping her chin with a thoughtful finger. She turned to Scarlett and Crimson. "Oh well! When you're identical twins and you spend all your time together, I guess it's only natural to get confused."

"You could always look at the name written on your undies," joked Kimono.

"You can't always trust that," Uniform said primly. "I really doubt someone would name a child 'Wash in Warm Water.'"

The twins continued to debate who was who as Scarlett and Crimson, chuckling in amusement at the sisters' confusion of identities, split up and checked the rooms out for new stuff. They passed a good hour this way and worried about the contest only every other minute instead of all the time. Finally Scarlett brought a large piece of lace tablecloth up to the sisters.

"Wonderful choice," said Kimono. "What do you plan to do with it?"

"I'm thinking of dyeing it black, shredding the fringes, and using it as a sort of spiderweb shawl," Scarlett replied.

"Sounds cool," said Crimson as she came up to the desk.

"How much?" Scarlett asked.

The twins looked at each other and silently communicated. "Tell you what, darlings," Kimono began. "We like your designs so much that we want to see them real."

"So take the lace, free," Uniform continued. "And help yourselves to whatever other fabrics you might need. All we want in return is that you use it all to make an outfit that we can put in the show window. And if . . . no, *when* it sells, we'll take half of that money as payback for advancing you materials."

"How does that sound?" Kimono finished.

Both Crimson and Scarlett were blown away by this generosity, not to mention the rush they felt in imagining selling one of their designs. "S-sure!" Scarlett stammered. "That sounds great!"

They left the store and walked home in a happy daze, chattering about which designs they should tackle first and what kind of materials they should use and who should do what work on the project. It wasn't until they split up at the mine entrance that Crimson realized they hadn't even thought about the demo, much less worried about it, for more than an hour. Great!

Too bad a whole long night still lay ahead. . . . And what a long night it would be.

SATURDAY

The auditorium was packed to standing room only. Kids from all over had shown up to hear the new music, hoping against hope that some of it might be unexpectedly cool. If such a gem appeared, it would be quickly labeled a "must-have" goodie and become a scene hit throughout the whole school district.

As soon as Scarlett and Crimson entered, followed by Pepper, Winslow, and the rest of the posse, they felt the eye-daggers thrown their way before they actually spotted the Leetz pack. Brianna and friends had brought an entire fan club with them, mostly

jocks who were more fans of the girls than their music.
To celebrate their expected win, the Leetz had come
dressed to the hilt in what they imagined their stage
outfits would look like. That is, they had rustled up
some old cheerleader uniforms and ironed on patches
that advertised their band name, the Queen Beez. They
had also found and distributed tiny pink pom-poms to
their posse, girls and boys alike. The girls were practicing
a cheer in a whisper, while the jock guys held their
pom-poms in limp embarrassment.

"Thank you all for coming," boomed Ms. Chelle's voice from the PA system. "V. Price Memorial Middle School is proud to be hosting this exciting event. We will be announcing the ten finalists, and playing their demos for all of you to hear. Please remember that this order is arbitrary. And special thanks to all those who submitted their work. Let's give them a cheer." The auditorium filled with polite applause—except from the Leetz crowd, who sat stone-faced and silent.

The curtains of the stage opened to reveal Ms.

Chelle standing in front of a table where three strangers sat. "First, let me introduce you to my fellow judges. Mrs. Creegan teaches music at her home, while Mr. Page and Mr. Robertson are professional musicians. Second, from all of the submissions, we chose the best ten songs as finalists. Songs were judged for performance, arrangement, and originality. Additional points were added or subtracted for engineering."

She picked up a clipboard and began reading from it. The first five demos seemed to fly by in a flash. With every announcement Scarlett and Crimson grew more and more nervous—now there were only five spots left to fill.

"Next up we have Terry, Teri, & Toni doing their original song, 'Shout Shout Shout.'" At her signal the speakers started playing a hip-hoppy rhythm. When the vocals kicked in, Scarlett and Crimson looked at each other in dismay. The performance was almost good enough to be called bad. The vocalists kept time but were obviously tone-deaf. At least it was an original.

"And from our very own V. Price Memorial, the Queen Beez's cover of 'You Can't Prove I Did It.'" A poppy dance lick repeated over and over while the Leetz girls tried to sing in harmony. At the first note of their

song, the Leetz pack let out a cheer—the guys shouting enthusiastically, some even waving their pom-poms.

The cheers quickly petered out. The performance was okay enough, but the demo seemed to have been recorded through a tin can.

"My bad," said Winslow from behind Brianna. The Leetz whirled around to stare. "I guess when I erased Scarlett and Crimson's song, I accidentally erased the final mix of yours. That's what you really sound like."

Brianna, Paige, and the others stood frozen in shock as their raw music drew to a close. Around them, the crowd of supporters melted away, leaving the girls alone and surrounded by dropped pom-poms.

Pepper gave Winslow a high five as he came back to the group. This time, Winslow's palm hit Pepper's with good timing. Scarlett and Crimson barely noticed.

"Those two songs were so lame," Scarlett said, "I'm starting to doubt the judges' judgment."

"Shh," hissed Crimson. "We did our best. It's gotta pay off."

But that didn't seem likely as the next two spots were awarded to two current hits—Bus Fare Hike playing "Diggin' Down 2 the Bottom" and Mopeless's rework of "Why Should I?" as a crunk jam.

"That's way more cover songs than originals," fretted Scarlett. "Do the judges think that originals are weaker than cover tunes?"

Crimson didn't answer, even when her girlfriend's hands gripped her arms in support and Pepper and Winslow both threw her thumbs-up.

"And last but certainly not least . . . ," Ms. Chelle began. "Well, all I can say is I've never heard anything like it—and I love it." Behind her the judges nodded in agreement. "It scored high in all the categories—

performance, arrangement, and especially, originality. That it was a near-perfect recording was only the icing on the cake for all of us judges. I give you—"

Scarlett and Crimson hardly noticed that they'd both stopped breathing.

"Once again from V. Price Memorial, DarqStarz doing 'A Light in the Darq'!"

The sound that came from the speakers began as a lonely organ theme in a vast space that felt the size of Carnegie (or Albert) Hall. When the chunky chorus kicked in, it was like a full-body penetration of sound.

The crowd listened entranced, and by the end of the song everyone was singing along with the chorus.

Scarlett and Crimson felt like they were standing in the thin air of a high mountain peak. Dumbstruck grins spread across their faces as they watched the crowd respond. Even the judges were tapping their feet. When the song ended and the entire auditorium exploded in applause, they didn't even hear their own shouts of joy over the deafening hooting and whistles.

It took Ms. Chelle a couple of minutes to bring the room back to order. When things quieted down, Crimson noticed that Brianna and the Leetz had vanished.

"As exciting as all this has been," said Ms. Chelle, "there's more excitement to come. In the next stage these ten finalists will play their songs live to compete for the number-one spot. You will have two weeks to prepare for the Halloween Battle of the Bands at the rec center. Good luck to you all."

Although it was near midnight, Scarlett sat in front of the computer in the Lair.

**DarqChat with Scarlett and Crimson
@ 11:52 p.m. on Saturday**

S U can't sleep either, Cee?

C Maybe I'll sleep when the shock wears off.
Or when the vibrating stops.

S Did U see the # of hits on R DarqSpace site?

C Yeah. Did U see that we've had over 100
downloads of R song? Ppl rly like it!!

S I never thought that R site would take off so
fast. There R lots of requests 2 join R chat room.
We owe a big shout-out 2 Pepper.

C & 2 Winslow, don't 4get. 2gether they made us
sound great. But we can't stop & rest yet. U
know what's next, don't U?

S I can think of lots of things. Tell me.

C My dad always says that the reward 4 doing a
good job is—

DarqChat with Scarlett and Crimson
@ 12:03 a.m. on Sunday

S Another job. I've only heard it like 1 million X. My mom & dad both say it 2.

C Well R next job is 2 put 2gether a band 2 play at the B o B.

S Can't I have just 1 day 2 enjoy this 1st? Pretty please?

C Sure. I guess U deserve it.

S WE deserve it. And we're gonna ace that Battle of the Bands 2, Cee–2gether!

C 4 ever, Ess! Go rest. Talk 2 U 2morrow. Love U.

S Love U right back. Night.

The next Darq tale is here . . .

A Light in the Darq

by Allyson Black
illustrated by Shane L. Johnson

SUNDAY Afternoon

"We're going to play in front of a *live* audience!" Scarlett Ravencraft and Crimson Hawthorne shrieked in unison. They pogoed up and down on the throw-rug-covered floor until the red streak in Scarlett's dark hair looked like a fan and Crimson's braids came loose.

"This. Is. So. Totally. *Awesome!*" they yelled over and over.

They were in the Lair, their own special room deep under Scarlett's house. Barely half a day before, their brand-new band, DarqStarz, was a finalist in the demo contest, which was the first part of their school district's

Battle of the Bands. Starting from scratch and against all odds, the girls had found the musical friends they needed to create the band, rehearse a song, and record a professional-sounding track.

Coming up with a song was no problem. Crimson had already written songs about their new scene: Darq. Darq was their point of view on the world and how to handle its challenges, and it was reflected in the style of music, clothes, and ideas that Scarlett and Crimson knew would speak to many people.

They had chosen a song that best expressed their deepest feelings, one called "A Light in the Darq." They secretly considered it the Darq anthem, and they'd been positive they could record a winning demo track that would speak to everyone.

Then into the mix had come a cool transfer student named Pepper White. As a fresh face, Pepper would have been a real prize for whichever scene grabbed him first. The top contenders in this contest were the Leetz, a clique of popular girls who went after Pepper like a swarm of bees, led by their queen, Brianna Morgan.

But Pepper was already friends with Winslow Leek, whose shy, geeky looks hid a supersharp mind. Winslow knew which musician played which instrument in just about any band Pepper could name, and he always carried around a laptop for editing sounds. He called it "sound sculpting."

When Pepper suggested that Winslow be a part of the Leetz as well, Brianna had dismissed Winslow with a sneered "Eww!"

Unimpressed with her reaction, Pepper had let Winslow lead him to Scarlett and Crimson. Because of Pepper's taste in bands and keyboard skills, he clicked with the girls immediately. The four of them agreed to play together, calling their band DarqStarz.

Excited to now have a band, Scarlett and Crimson were ready to jump at any chance to express themselves musically. So when the school district announced a Battle of the Bands, the girls were all over it. Those who entered had to record a song as professionally as they could for the demo part of the competition. The song didn't have to be original, but the music had to be performed by the students themselves.

Scarlett, Crimson, Pepper, and Winslow had thrown themselves into the race by recording and mixing "A Light in the Darq" in less than a week.

In spite of the efforts of Brianna and the Leetz to sabotage DarqStarz, it seemed that the judges scored Scarlett and Crimson's crew higher than the Leetz's band, the Queen Beez. As their prize, the ten top-scoring bands—DarqStarz, the Queen Beez, and eight others— were given the next level's challenge. Each band had to perform their song before judges and a live audience on Halloween, barely two weeks away.

Crimson, of course, was more than up for the challenge. "We're going to rock Old Mill like it's never been rocked!" she declared, as the girls and Pepper chilled out in the Lair.

"Play it again, Pepper," Scarlett called out.

Pepper lay upside down on his back in a big beanbag chair. He stuck a skinny arm straight up and clicked the remote control in his hand.

The stirring sounds of DarqStarz's "A Light in the Darq" filled the Lair for the seventh time. Airy acoustic fingerpicking floated the lines of the verses, then crashing, slashing power chords hammered home the defiant chorus.

Be your own scene. Be your own scene.

Who are you when you're all alone in the Darq?
Nothing but you and your own beating heart?

Be your own scene. Be your own scene.

Without all the glam and the gear and the fear,
They'll see that you're just too smart.

Be your own scene. Be your own scene.

To follow the fish as they all school away,
Turning "blend in" into some kind of art.

Be your own scene. Be your own scene.
Be your own scene. Be your own scene.
You know you've got the skill,
And you sure deserve the thrill,
By now you know the drill . . .
Be your own scene.

Crimson bippity-bopped along with the music on an invisible drum kit while Scarlett rocked out on electric air guitar. Pepper's fingers pantomimed his keyboard playing. Then Scarlett strutted the room for her silent solo. Matching Scarlett's energy, Crimson jumped up and began hammering away at a ring of invisible cymbals around her head.

Challenged to pump it up, Scarlett began adding head-banging lunges across the Lair to her prancing. The girls got more and more into the music until the giggles made them collapse to the floor when the song ended. On their backs and panting, they both called to Pepper, "Again! Play it again!"

But instead of playing the song again, Pepper announced in his clipped English accent, "It's not going to work, you know."

Scarlett looked confused. Crimson tilted her head to one side and asked cautiously, *"What's* not going to work?"

"Playing 'A Light in the Darq' that way live," Pepper said, as if it were the most obvious thing in the world.

Scarlett's jaw set. "What's not to work?" she demanded. "We've got the gear, we have the skills, and most important, we have the whole Darq thing to keep us focused."

"All true," Pepper admitted. "But we don't have enough players to re-create that exact sound. We did a *lot* of overdubs to fill out the Darq vibe on tape. To play that sound live, we need another player. An ace one."

Scarlett was stunned. "Find a stranger? Who already feels the Darq vibe, even though we just created it? With, like, a deadline of two weeks even if we started, like, five minutes ago?" She sank into an overstuffed chair and sighed loudly. "Well, *that's* a humongous sack of ain't-gonna-happen!"

"You know better than that, Ravencraft," Pepper said, heaving himself out of the beanbag. "We tackle big challenges by breaking them down into doable bits, don't we? If we're going to advertise, we ought to decide exactly what we're looking for."

Scarlett stared blankly at the ceiling. Crimson's face was set in serious thought. Pepper finally jumped into the silence. "First skill, vocals," he began, raising three fingers of one hand and tapping each one in turn. "Ravencraft, you're a soprano. Hawthorne, you're an alto. I'm a tenor. So the obvious harmony gap is . . ."

"Bass," Scarlett answered automatically. "I remember now. We faked that by using tech to shift your voice down an octave."

Pepper nodded. "See? We just knocked off anyone who can't sing bass from our search. That's one chunk out of the way." Tapping a second finger, he said, "Next: The biggest cheats we did were instrumental overdubs to fill out the sound. Now, Ravencraft can cover guitar, 'cause it's, like, the root of your sound. As far as the bass goes, I can cover that with my keyboard. But the keyboard can't duplicate Hawthorne's slap-bass thing. We need either a bassist or a drummer."

Pepper turned to Crimson. "You played both, you get first pick."

"Drums!" Crimson exclaimed without hesitation. She did a fancy roll on air drums and smashed an invisible cymbal. "Bang-bang, thump-thump, straight from the gut. Pure, primitive. Gimme, gimme."

"Another chunk aced," said Pepper. "We might as well look for a guy who can do both. Any names pop up?"

Scarlett and Crimson looked at each other and shook their heads. "All the good guys are already into different scenes," Scarlett said.

Pepper pulled some folded papers from the back pocket of his jeans and tossed them into Scarlett's lap. "Well, I scanned the school's social net, searching for likelies. Here are five. Have a look. Only you can judge who would get the whole Darq vibe. As for me, I've got to go. I'm off to Leek's to help with a problem."

Pepper turned and walked down the tunnel and out the delivery door. The path beyond the door snaked up to Crimson's backyard. Pepper's house was just a few streets beyond that.

Back in the Lair, a thick silence filled the room. The two best friends sat leaning back-to-back for several minutes, thinking hard. How would they find a hot bass player who would get their whole Darq scene?

"This is serious overloadage for me, Cee," Scarlett said. "You're the deep one. How do we pick a stranger to join us?"

"Not a clue, Ess," replied Crimson. "But when have I ever let a little thing like *that* stop me?"